AF583584

AUSTRALIA
is our home

by Laura Giuffrida

illustrated by Julia Chapman

Published by
Book Ink Pty Ltd
P O Box 1020
Castlemaine VIC 3450

bookink.net.au

This book was produced in Castlemaine using environmentally friendly inks and paper (www.printtogether.com.au)

ISBN: 9780648459309

A catalogue record for this book is available from the National Library of Australia

I wrote this story over ten years ago, when children seeking asylum with their families was an important issue, one we are still talking about today. This book is dedicated to all of the children who call Australia their home, and to those still waiting.
And to my own children, who inspire me every day.

Laura

-

Many thanks and much love to my family, Mal and Jess the Border Collie for their encouragement and support.
Also thank you to Laura for giving me the opportunity to bring her wonderful story to life on the page.

Julia

Belle is from Australia.
She's from a farm near Ruffy.
She loves collecting chicken's eggs
and playing with her puppy.

tea
GARDENING TODAY
NEWS
TRENDS
hello
FOOTBALL REVIEW
DOGS!
Coffee
Latte $
espresso
Food
Bagels
Muffins

Charlie came from Bangladesh.
They had a market stall.
Now his family has a shop!
He loves to play football.

Piesta is from Afghanistan.
Her village had no school.
Now she's having lessons
at the local swimming pool.

VEGEMITE

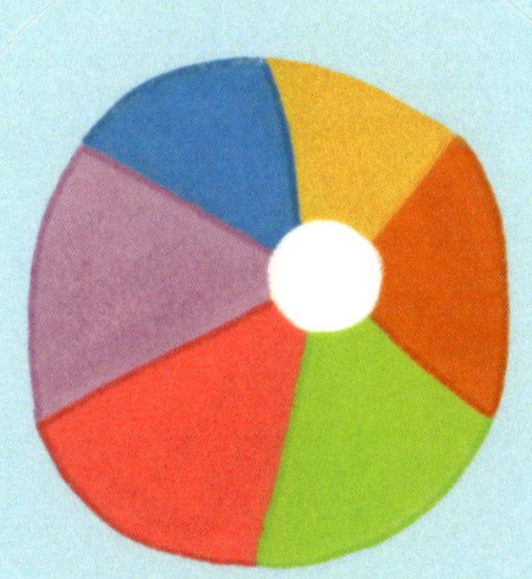

BOOK INK
PUBLISHING

Hank came from America
Where they speak English too.
Though togs are trunks, and autumn's fall
They speak like me and you!

LVIEW
RY SCHOOL
EWS—

Bo-lin is from China,
born in Shanghai, on the coast.
Now she lives in Melbourne;
she loves vegemite on toast.

Wantak is from Africa,
born in the Sudan.
His parents travelled many miles
To bring him to this land.

STUV
WXYZ

Giovanni is from Italy.
His family there is big.
He likes to go to kinder
to play with the guinea pig.

Sofea is from Singapore.
That's not too far away.
You should have heard her parents laugh
when she first said 'g'day!'

William is from England
where they eat a food called kippers.
His favourite thing on weekends
is to swim and splash at nippers!

Akira is from Japan.
She lived amongst the towers.
Now she has a cubby house
and lots of tree and flowers.

Neerim is from Arnhem Land.
His mob's been there a while.
When he went camping with his dad
they saw a crocodile!

We all live in Australia.
Australia is our home.
We make our country special.
We make this land our own.

VEGEMITE
VEGEMITE
VEGEMITE